Random Kindness & Senseless Acts of Beauty

Written by Anne Herbert & Margaret Paloma Pavel

Illustrated by Mayumi Oda

Foreword by Desmond Tutu

New Village Press, New York

Published in the United States by
New Village Press
bookorders@newvillagepress.net
www.newvillagepress.net

Manufactured in China

ISBN 978-1-61332-015-0
Publication Date: September 30, 2014

Library of Congress Cataloging-in-Publication Data

Herbert, Anne.
  Random kindness and senseless acts of beauty / written by Anne Herbert & Margaret
Paloma Pavel ; illustrated by Mayumi Oda ; foreword by Desmond Tutu. -- first [edi-
tion].
      pages cm
  Summary: "Humans are depicted as animals who show how survival is tied to choices
for either violence or compassion. The theme is that every person has the power to create peace and joy in the world through simple actions"-- Provided by publisher.
   ISBN 978-1-61332-015-0 (alk. paper)
  1. Kindness. I. Pavel, Margaret M. II. Title.
  BJ1533.K5H47 2014
  177.7--dc23
                         2014023756

Foreword

We are living in an historic moment. We are each called to take part in a great transformation. Our survival as a species is threatened by global warming, economic meltdown, and an ever-increasing gap between rich and poor. Yet these threats offer an opportunity to awaken as an interconnected and beloved community.

Here in South Africa, interconnectedness is described by the concept ubuntu. Ubuntu is the philosophy and belief that our humanity is inextricably bound up in one another, and any tear in the fabric of connection must be repaired for us all to be made whole. This interconnectedness is the very root of who we are. Thus, compassion and service to others enhances the humanity of all, including oneself. As South Africa overcame the trauma of Apartheid, we discovered that ubuntu builds extraordinary resilience, enabling our people to survive and emerge still human despite all efforts to dehumanize our community.

Ubuntu tells us that we can create a more peaceful world by striving for goodness in each moment, wherever we are. Thus we are invited to become life artists, those who create lives of wholeness and beauty at every instant. Out of the cacophony of random suffering and chaos that can mark human life, the life artist sees or creates a symphony of meaning and order. A life of wholeness does not depend on what we experience, but on how we experience our lives.

My conviction that this is true is borne out not only by my experiences in South Africa, where we miraculously averted a bloodbath by cultivating forgiveness over cycles of retribution and violence, but also by many visits to other countries suffering oppression and conflict. We can indeed transform the world, and we are each called to take part in this sacred work.

Random Kindness and Senseless Acts of Beauty offers this simple and powerful message of wisdom and hope. Wherever we are, we can create beauty. Moment by moment, we can create joy. Instant by instant, we can offer kindness.

—Desmond Mpilo Tutu, Soweto, 2014

Random Kindness & Senseless Acts of Beauty

Our leaders got confused.

So . . .

we're all leaders now.

They told us there
was nothing we
could do.

They were wrong.

When we
tell ourselves
there is
nothing we
can do,

We are wrong.

We never know how much,
and we never know how far it goes,

But always
we have power.

We have power

*We're all making the soup
we're all eating.*

We're all weaving the cloth
we're all wearing.

What we do can't go away.

We are all in the circle together.

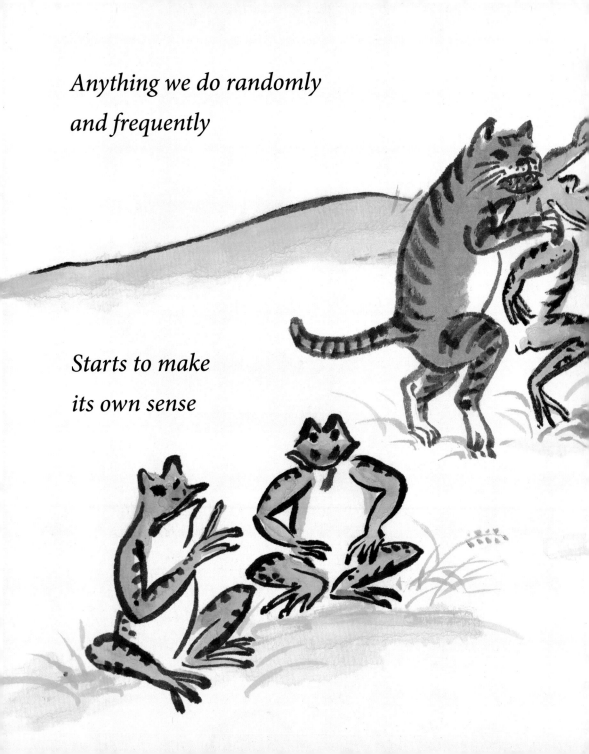

Anything we do randomly

and frequently

Starts to make

its own sense

And changes the world

into itself.

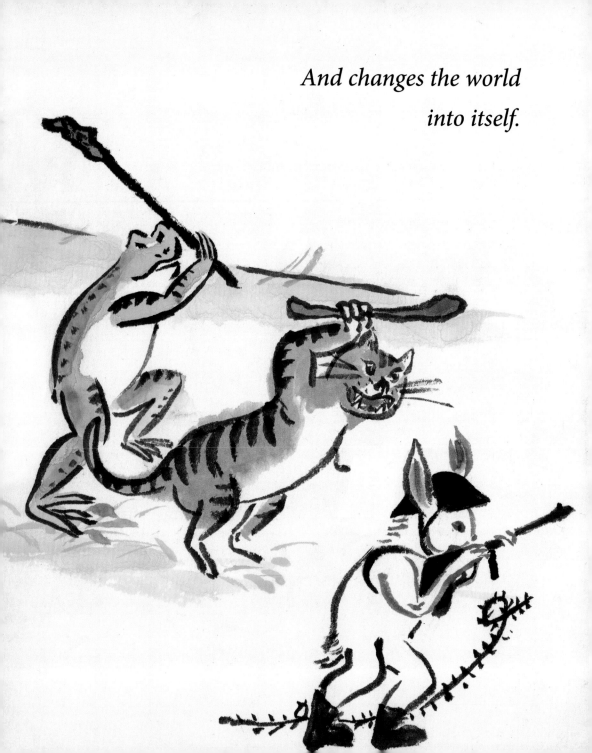

Senseless violence makes

more and more sense,

when vengeance and fear

*Take us
closer and
closer to a world
where everyone
is dead
for no reason.*

But violence isn't the only thing

that is senseless

until it makes its own sense.

Anything you want there to be more of,

Do it randomly.

Don't wait for reasons.

*It will make itself
be more
senselessly.*

Scrawl it on the wall—

Random Kindness and Senseless Acts of Beauty!

*We are right on the edge
of discovering
millions of new ways
of being together,*

*Millions of
new dances*

*we can
do together
minute by minute.*

*And we're right on the edge of
destroying ourselves out of life,*

Because we are too scared to have that much delight.

We're right on the edge.

The steps we take now
make new earth grow
beneath our feet.

*The steps
we take now
decide
what kind
of earth that
will be.*

In every moment

we live

we have the choice

*to find the fight
or make
delight.*

We have Power.

It's a circle.

Start the dance.

It is my great joy to know this twentieth-anniversary edition of *Random Kindness and Senseless Acts of Beauty* will support community resilience throughout the world. The first edition of this book was published to break the spell of war, random violence and senseless acts of cruelty. Now, as our population has increased and our commonwealth of earth, air, and water are seriously threatened, the call to link arms and lay down armaments is more urgent than ever. With this edition we invite you to join the Random Kindness Community Resilience Project. Together we can make a new earth grow.

I am grateful Anne Herbert's phrase from 1982—Practice random kindness and senseless acts of beauty—has proliferated worldwide. It is a testament to her poetic wisdom. May we take to heart the message that every action makes a difference in an inextricably connected world.

— *M. Paloma Pavel, Oakland, California*

When Anne Herbert and Margaret Paloma Pavel approached me to illustrate this beautiful story, I had been working as an antinuclear activist in Japan and the United States. I felt strongly drawn to this message and poured my emotions onto the images, creating a pictorial complement that drew from my experiences with our world and my work as an activist. I based my design on the 12th Century Japanese scroll—*Birds and Animals Frolicking.*

My original art for the book was painted in black and red. In early 2011, I felt compelled to turn my illustrations into color, breathing new life into the story. I was deeply immersed in this venture when the tragic earthquake and tsunami struck on March 11, 2011. I was in Nara, Japan, at that time working with traditional scroll-maker Mr. Shosaku Yoshimura. It was there I knew this timely story had to be told, once again, to the new generations that will care for this planet.

I dedicate this scroll to every child of the Earth.

— *Mayumi Oda, Kealakekua, Hawaii*

This edition of *Random Kindness*, with new full-color illustrations by artist Mayumi Oda and a new foreword by the honorable Desmond Tutu, is dedicated to peace and recovery in the face of world unrest and climate crises. Please visit www.RandomKindnessProject.org to bring the Random Kindness Community Resilience Project to your community.

All royalties from the sale of this book will be donated to antinuclear advocacy and community resiliency across boundaries.

Anne Herbert is an American writer and past assistant editor of *CoEvolution Quarterly*. She is known for authoring the expression, "Practice random kindness and senseless acts of beauty."

Margaret Paloma Pavel is an educator, psychologist, and international advocate of healthy, just, and resilient urban communities. She is founder and president of Earth House Center in Oakland, California, and editor of *Breakthrough Communities: Sustainability and Justice in the Next American Metropolis* (MIT Press).

Mayumi Oda is a global activist and revered artist known as the "Matisse of Japan." She has illustrated the books of the esteemed Buddhist monk Thich Nhat Hanh and exhibited over fifty one-woman shows throughout the world.

Desmond Mpilo Tutu is Archbishop Emeritus of Cape Town South Africa and world renowned social rights activist. He is recipient of the Nobel Peace Prize, the Albert Schweitzer Prize for Humanitarianism, the Pacem in Terris Award, the Sydney Peace Prize, and the Gandhi Peace Prize.